Check (
✔ STE(

Get reac

~~SNAKE RIVER~~

Where there's smoke. . . there's fire
Read all about it in
SMOKE

Is there any truth to the old pirate's poem?
Find out in
FORGOTTEN TREASURE

Are they tough enough to rough it?
Check out the boys who
DON'T LOOK BACK

They're burning rubber in the desert heat!
See who in
ROAD RALLY

Danger lies where eagles soar. Find out why in
SOARING SUMMER

Knight makes right? See how in
KNIGHT MOVES

The chase is on — but who's hunting who?
Find out, read
DANGEROUS GAME

A family can survive anything, right?
Learn more in
SNOW TREK

ISBN 0-8114-9315-6

3 4 5 6 7 8 9 98

Produced by Mega-Books of New York, Inc.
Design and Art Direction by Michaelis/Carpelis Design Assoc.

Cover illustration: Don Morrison

VIDEO QUEST

by William McCay

interior illustrations by
Frank Mayo

STECK-VAUGHN
C O M P A N Y

CHAPTER ONE

"Just two weeks until spring vacation!" Tina Rowan smiled as she put down her lunch tray. Not even the food at William T. Sherman High School could spoil her mood.

Wilson Chu patted a seat beside him at the lunchroom table where two of Tina's other friends, Tommy Colon and Pablo Lazarus, also sat. They all dug into their lunches.

Just then Annie Harker came rushing up with a newspaper in her hands. "Check out this headline, guys!"

"'TV Station Runs Contest,'" Wilson read out loud. "What's the contest?"

"It's run by WQSN," Annie said. "They call it the Video Quest. Teams get six hours to shoot the six most interesting places in town. The winners get a prize, and their videotape is shown on TV." She smiled. "You want to give it a try?"

"Sounds cool to me," said Wilson. He pointed to Tina. "Besides, we've got a great camera person right here."

"Oh, come on," Tina blushed.

"Hey, I saw the tape you made of your brother's wedding," Wilson said. "It was great!"

Tina sighed. "I shot that with my brother's video camera. He took it with him when he moved."

Annie frowned. "I don't have a video camera, either."

"Don't look at me," Wilson shrugged. "Those things cost money."

"I bet I could get one," Tommy said. His dad's store sold TVs, radios, and video cameras.

"That would really save the day," Annie said. But she didn't sound too happy. Tommy was new at school, nice enough, but so far he seemed a bit bossy. If they used his camera, he might want to run the whole show.

Tina looked at Annie. Annie looked at Wilson. "So, it looks like we've got a camera," Wilson said with a shrug.

"I can help, too," Pablo offered. "I've

finally got my car running again."

"How many months did it take you to fix it?" Wilson joked.

Pablo had worked for a year at three different jobs to buy a car. A month after he'd bought it, the car had died right in his driveway.

"Don't knock my wheels," Pablo told Wilson. "They'll take you where you want to go," he said. "After all, you only have six hours."

"You're right," said Wilson. Then he smiled at Tina, Pablo, and Annie. "It will take teamwork if we want our tape to be a winner."

"Yeah, yeah," Tommy cut in. "Now we need six places to tape. And I know just where we should go."

Annie jumped in. "I think we all should make lists," she said. "After all, five heads are better than one."

Tommy gave her a dirty look, but he stayed quiet as Annie continued. "Let's

meet at Burger World after school.
Everybody bring a list."

That afternoon, when Tina walked
into the burger shop, Wilson was
already there. "Got your list?" he asked.

She handed him a sheet of paper.

"Rainbow Park," Wilson read. "I
chose that, too." He went down the list,
then looked puzzled. "What's this you
wrote about flags?"

"I thought we could claim each place

we tape with a flag," Tina said. "That way each of us would have a reason to get in front of the camera."

"Well, there are five people on the team and six places to shoot," Wilson grinned. "I guess we can even let Tommy go twice!"

Tina giggled as Tommy ran in waving a crumpled piece of paper. "Check these places out!" he said proudly.

Pablo and Annie came in behind him. Annie read over Tommy's shoulder. "The

city morgue? Gross! That's where they keep all the dead people!"

As Annie continued to read, she began to laugh. "You want to go to the top of Harborside Bridge? Pablo drives a car, not a helicopter!"

"What's the problem?" Tommy asked.

"We only have six hours for shooting," Annie explained. "Your list would take two days! We probably can't even get into some of these places. It would be against the law."

Tommy's voice grew loud. "You'd better take some of my ideas. I'm getting you the camera, after all." He frowned at the other kids. "Don't think you can blow me off. Or I might just blow off this whole thing!"

CHAPTER TWO

Two Saturdays later, it was contest day. Tina and her friends stood outside the offices of WQSN. The big clock on the building was about to strike noon.

Twenty teams listened as Ed Hanley, a local newsman for WQSN, went over the rules. "Starting at twelve o'clock, you'll begin taping. It's against contest policy for you to break any laws or put yourselves in danger, so be careful. I'll be waiting here at six o'clock tonight to pick up your tapes."

Tina glanced at the group's list for the tenth time.

"Ready, set . . . go!" Mr. Hanley cried.

The teams went charging off. Tina and her friends ran to Pablo's car.

"First stop, Rainbow Park!" Annie said as she jumped inside. "Is the camera ready?"

Everybody except Tommy had agreed that Annie would be their "producer."

After all, entering the contest had been her idea.

Tommy patted the bag on his lap. "It's ready and loaded. I took care of it myself."

"Tina, could you double-check it?" Annie asked. "We don't want find out we forgot to load the tape."

Tina took the camera. "It's all set up," she said. Just then they reached the park.

"Why don't you shoot this scene, Tina?" Annie said. "You've already got the camera." Annie didn't look at Tommy as she opened the car door.

But Tommy burst out of the car right behind her. "What's the big idea?" he yelled. "First you pick wimpy stuff to tape. Then you choose hardly any of the cool places on my list. Now you think you can cut me out of shooting? I'm the one who got the stupid camera!"

"It's not that way," Annie said. "Tina's

just really good at shooting."

"It's my camera!" Tommy cried.

"Maybe we can do it together," Tina suggested.

"Sure," Tommy said nastily. "I'll aim, and you can focus."

"How about I shoot, but you pick the shot?" Tina smiled at Tommy.

Tommy gave a shrug. "So who's planting the first flag?"

"How about Pablo?" Wilson asked.

"Then let's go," said Tommy. He stomped his way through the gates. "We've wasted enough time arguing."

The gang followed Tommy to the middle of the park. He leaned against a big tree.

"What kind of angle should we go for?" Tina asked.

"Let's climb this tree," Tommy said. "We'll catch Pablo from above."

Tina slipped the camera's strap around her neck. She grabbed hold of the tree trunk and pulled herself up. Tommy came right after her.

"I think this is high enough," said Tina as she looked down from halfway up the tree.

"Are you kidding?" Tommy gave a nasty laugh. "You've got to go to the top of the tree. Don't you know why they call this Rainbow Park?"

Tina stared down. "Great," she thought. "I'm fifteen, and I've just found

out I'm scared of heights." She braced herself and climbed higher. Then she began to understand. In each corner of the park, flowers had been planted in rows of arches. Each row of flowers was a different color. There were red, orange, yellow, green, light blue, dark blue, and purple arches. Seen from above, the flower beds looked just like a rainbow!

"Now I see what you mean," Tina exclaimed.

"You still have to go higher to get the whole thing," Tommy said to her from a lower branch. "If you're scared, I'll do it myself."

"No, I can handle it," answered Tina. She scrambled from branch to branch. The higher she climbed, the thinner the branches became.

At last Tina sat herself down on one of the highest branches. "Okay, Pablo!" she shouted down. "Go to the flowers over to the left there!"

Pablo walked to one of the rainbow flower beds, waving their team flag.

"Okay," Tina called. "Plant our flag . . . Good! Now step back and spread your arms wide. Give me a smile!"

Tina zoomed in on Pablo with the

camera lens. Then she pulled the lens away. She twisted around on her branch, taking in the whole park.

"Oh, no!" Tommy's voice came from below. "Check out the main gate!"

Tina stopped taping and looked. A bunch of kids ran into the garden. One

carried a video camera.

"It's another team coming to shoot here," Tommy said with disgust. "I told you this was a bad choice!"

But Tina had worse problems on her mind. She felt the branch beneath her beginning to bend. Then it made a loud cracking noise.

Before Tina could move, the branch snapped in two!

CHAPTER THREE

Tina screamed as she fell. Then a hand grabbed her belt. "Hold onto the camera!" Tommy yelled in her ear.

For a second, Tina seemed to bounce in midair. She grabbed for the tree trunk with one hand. Her other hand gripped the camera. Then Tina managed to clamber onto a sturdy branch.

"Are you okay?" Tommy asked. "Man, that was lucky! My dad would have killed me if the camera had broken."

"What about me?" Tina snapped. "I wouldn't have felt too cool hitting the ground."

"Yeah, well," Tommy said, not looking at her. "You see, my dad doesn't exactly know I have the camera. I sort of borrowed it from the store."

"So you saved me to save the camera." Tina shook her head. "You're a real piece of work, Tommy Colon!"

Neither Tina nor Tommy spoke as they climbed down to the others.

"Let's go," Wilson said. "Time is ticking away."

"Okay," said Annie, looking at her list. "The next spot to shoot—"

"Is just a couple of blocks away," Tommy interrupted. "I chose St. John's Church. So I get to do the taping this time." He gave Annie a hard stare.

"All right," she shrugged.

"Why did you pick St. John's?" asked Pablo.

"Hey, it's cool," Tommy told his friend. "We're filming under the church, in the crypt!"

"The crib?" Pablo asked.

Tommy laughed. "Close. But babies sleep in cribs. When you're in a crypt, you sleep forever."

"A crypt is a burial vault," Annie explained.

"We're going down where they bury people?" Pablo stared at Tommy.

"Hey, it's not like there will be vampires walking around," Tommy said. "It's just a dark, spooky place. And I'll bet nobody else will go taping there."

The gang got into Pablo's car and drove to St. John's Church. It was a huge, old-fashioned building.

"We can get in over here," said Tommy. He led the others down a side street. "They finished building the church in 1900. But the cellars go back 200 years!"

He stopped at a short wooden door in the middle of the block. Tommy yanked on the handle till the old door creaked

open. Tina shivered. It was the kind of sound she usually heard in horror movies.

Annie peered through the doorway to a set of stone steps that went down into the darkness. "You're sure this is all right?" she asked Tommy. "You checked in with the people at the church?"

"Sure, sure," Tommy said. "They left

the doors unlocked, didn't they? Come
on. The sooner we start shooting, the
sooner we'll be finished."

He carried the camera down the
stairs. Pablo followed with a bag of
supplies from the car. Tommy reached
into the bag and pulled out a flashlight.
He aimed the beam of light around as
the others came down.

"What did I tell you?" Tommy grinned. "Is this cool or what?"

The flashlight picked out thick, square pillars. Thick wooden beams ran along the ceiling. Spider webs hung everywhere. Against the wall, Tina could make out big stone boxes.

Then she realized with another shiver that those weren't just boxes. They were coffins! Tina gulped.

"It's kind of dark to shoot any tape in here," she whispered.

"I thought of that," said Tommy. He reached into the supply bag and pulled out a bundle of white candles. "We'll stick these around to brighten things up. It will look good and spooky."

"I'm not going near any spiders," Pablo said. Then he pointed to a corner. "Is that a rat?"

"Where?" Tommy jumped. Then he looked closer. "It's just a ball of dust," he said with relief.

Tina, Annie, and Wilson set up the candles while Tommy prepared the camera. Pablo held the flashlight, trying to make the area as bright as possible.

"We'll put the flag here," said Tommy. He pointed to a big marble slab. Someone's name had been carved on it, but years of dust and spiderwebs had covered the letters.

"Annie, you hold the flag this time," Tommy said. "Everyone else, get up on the stairs and out of the way."

Tommy aimed the camera at Annie, who knelt with the flag. She looked a little scared as she leaned it against the marble slab.

Suddenly they heard another door open. "What's going on down here?" a gruff voice demanded.

Annie jumped to her feet with a scream. A shadowy figure stood in a doorway at the far end of the cellar.

"What are you doing with those candles?" the man shouted. "Don't you know you could set the church on fire?"

The gang of friends didn't wait to hear more. They ran as if a hundred vampires were chasing them.

CHAPTER FOUR

The kids dashed out to Pablo's car and jumped in. They zoomed away as the man came out of the small church door.

When Annie finally caught her breath, she began yelling. "You didn't get permission to go in there, did you, Tommy?"

"Why bother?" he answered. "They might have said no."

"So you just walked right in and started setting fires," Annie accused him.

"I only lit a couple of candles," Tommy said. "It's no big deal. We got away, didn't we?"

"Oh, yeah?" Annie asked. "If we win, our tape will be on television. Whoever caught us down there will know it was us."

"Great," Wilson muttered. "We'll get a prize and get in trouble, too."

"You all worry too much," Tommy said. "What's next on the list?"

"The ferry," Annie said. She frowned as she looked at her watch. "That's going to take a lot of time. And we're running behind."

"Don't worry," Pablo told her. "I know a shortcut." Ten minutes later, Pablo parked his car at the ferry landing. Everyone jumped out to get ferry tickets. Tina talked to the ferryboat captain about setting up her shot.

She came back smiling. "It's okay," Tina said to her friends. "The crew will even help with the fishing line."

The ferry had two decks. One was for

passengers. The other held cars. Tina
and her friends were on the lower level,
where the cars were.

A crew member waved at them from
above. In one hand he held the roll of
fishing line Tina had given the captain.
The sailor tied the end of the line to the

top railing. Then he tossed the roll down. Wilson caught it and stretched the clear thread tight.

"Can you see it, Tina?" Wilson asked.

Tina was setting the camera up on its tripod. She looked through the viewer. Her guess was right. The fishing line was almost invisible!

"It's perfect!" she said.

By now the ferry was halfway across the river that ran through the city. The tall downtown buildings rose up behind them. Tina turned the camera, catching the whole skyline.

Then she aimed at Wilson, who stood beside the clear fishing line. He waved the team flag with a grin. Then he began tying the flag onto the line with a small piece of wire.

"Okay, the camera's lined up," Tina said. The fishing line was stretched in front of Webster Tower, the tallest building in town. The office tower was

actually a mile away.

But through the camera, it looked as though Wilson was tying a flag right onto the building's spire!

"A little higher, Wilson," Tina said, her eyes glued to the viewer. "Go right now, just hold it."

She frowned, rewinding the tape.

It took three tries to get it right. Luckily, the Captain kept the ferry moving slowly. "That's it!" Tina said happily. "The last shot was perfect!"

"It's about time," Tommy complained. "I thought you were going to use up all the videotape."

Tommy took the camera from Tina, checking the tape. The ferry began to slow. "Hey! We're docking!" said Tommy. He headed for the front of the ferryboat.

Above them, the sailor cut the knot on the fishing line. Wilson rolled up the loose line while Pablo folded away the tripod.

Annie kept frowning at her watch. "This is all taking too long." Her voice was worried.

Tommy was at the ferry railing when the others came up to him. "We won't have time to stay on and ride this ferry back," he said.

"But we've got to get to the library and the rare book room," Pablo said. "Taping the old comic books on display there will be cool."

"I've got a better plan," Tommy said. "There's a subway station close by. Instead of waiting for the ferry, we could take the subway train back to Pablo's car. That way we could shoot something else from my list."

"What?" Pablo asked. "A monster factory?"

Tommy gave Pablo a dirty look. "I was thinking about the lost subway station."

"How do you lose a subway station?" Wilson joked.

"It's not really lost," Tommy replied, annoyed. "It's just been closed for the last fifty years. You can see it in the dark if you know where to look. I've seen it riding by on the train. Come on."

Tommy leaped onto the dock and led the way to the subway station. After paying their fares, the others followed Tommy to the platform. Just then a

train pulled in and the group piled on.

The train arrived at Harborside Station, and Tommy was the first one off. The others trailed after him as he headed down the platform.

"Tommy, let's talk about this first," Wilson called to him. But Tommy wouldn't stop.

"Tommy!" Annie shouted angrily.

Tina, Wilson, Pablo, and Annie began to run after Tommy. But before they reached him he disappeared at the end of the platform.

Seconds later, the others reached the same spot. They found a metal ladder leading down to the tracks.

Beside it was a sign with big red letters. "NO PASSENGERS ALLOWED BEYOND THIS POINT BY ORDER OF LAW."

CHAPTER FIVE

The kids stood together in front of the sign. "I don't get it," Tina said. "First he takes the camera. Then he pushes into that church without asking. Now he's decided to break the law."

"Yeah, Tommy just keeps getting better and better." sighed Pablo. Even he was upset. "I'm the oldest, so I'll go get him. There's no sense in all of us getting in trouble."

Pablo climbed down the ladder. The others watched him walk along the wall of the tunnel, keeping away from the tracks. After ten steps, Pablo disappeared into the darkness.

There was nothing left for the remaining three to do but wait. Annie checked her watch. Tina and Wilson peeked down the tracks.

The train they'd ridden to Harborside Square was a local. It stopped at every station. But there were express trains on this line, too. Three expresses thundered by, one after another.

"What's keeping them?" Annie asked.

"I don't know about you," Wilson said. "But I wouldn't want to be near those tracks right now. There are too many trains whizzing past."

Another express rocketed through the station. Then another local train pulled up, letting passengers off.

The kids could only stand around and helplessly watch their time tick away.

Finally, Pablo came out of the tunnel. His face was pale and angry as he climbed onto the platform.

Behind him came Tommy, smiling

from ear to ear. "I got some great shots!" he said, waving the camera. "The lost station was dark. But I was able to use the lights from passing trains. In fact, I shot the trains as they zoomed by. And my pal here even had a flag to plant!"

"Don't call me your pal!" Pablo shouted. "The only reason I went there was to get you out. But no, you had to stay. Then we were stuck with all those trains rolling by. We had to flatten ourselves against the wall," Pablo growled.

"There's a little space in there for the subway track workers to step into when the trains pass," Tommy argued. "It's safe . . . besides, it was fun!"

"Maybe you had fun shooting. But standing around in the dark with a bunch of rats running around is not my idea of fun," Pablo shot back.

Tommy's mouth dropped open. "There were rats?"

"Yeah," Pablo said. "I guess you were too busy to notice."

Tommy just gulped.

"Well, we have a problem," Annie said. "We've still got to tape two places.

And there's only a little more than an hour left."

"Will the library still be open?" Tina asked.

Pablo sighed. "The library closes at five o'clock. Even if we jump in the car, we won't make it."

"So what are we going to shoot, Pablo

and his car?" asked Wilson.

Tina turned to Wilson. "Don't be such a . . . Hey! Where's Tommy?"

They all whipped around. Tommy and the camera were gone!

Annie stomped her foot. "Oh, man! What more can he do to us?"

"I'm afraid to ask," Tina said. "What places are left on his list?"

Annie shrugged. "Well, there's no place nearby, except . . . oh, no!"

"Where?" the others all asked.

"We're at Harborside Square," Annie said. "And Tommy wanted to shoot from the top of the Harborside Bridge."

"If he goes there . . ." Pablo began.

Wilson cut in. "We'll never be able to shoot another place by six o'clock!"

They dashed up the stairs. The Harborside Bridge was easy to find. They just followed the backed-up traffic.

"Look!" Pablo pointed at the bridge entrance. "The bridge is under repair."

Bulldozers and other machines blocked
one of the entrance ramps. But the five
o'clock whistle must have blown,
because there were no workers around.

"I'll bet Tommy walked right up that
ramp," Wilson said. "Let's check it out."

They all headed up the empty ramp.

Part of it had been torn up. Tina gave a nervous look at where the guard rails used to be.

"You don't think he'll really climb to the top of the tower, do you?" Wilson asked the others.

"There's a walkway that runs above the cables," Annie said. "But with all the work that's being done, I doubt Tommy could—"

"Oh yeah?" Pablo said. "Just look up there."

The other three looked to where Pablo pointed. A tall wooden ladder leaned against a steel pillar. The top of the ladder just reached a set of metal rungs in the pillar. A person could reach the walkway by climbing up the rungs. Tommy had just reached for the first metal rung.

When he saw the others, Tommy picked up the video camera that hung from his neck.

"Say cheese!" he yelled.

But as he turned to tape them, Tommy lost his balance. The other kids gasped. Tommy was falling!

CHAPTER SIX

Tina hid her face in her hands. Wilson and Annie turned away as Tommy screamed. Then there was silence.

Suddenly Pablo shouted, "Hey, guys! Look!" He was leaning over the side of the ramp. "Tommy!" he shouted. "You are one lucky dude!"

Tommy was only a few feet below them. He had landed on a big safety net. Now he lay on his back, staring up at his friends.

"Are you okay?" Wilson asked.

"Yeah," Tommy said. "Except that my father is going to kill me. I dropped the camera!"

Annie laughed. "Don't worry! The camera landed on the net, too. It's about two feet above your head and off to the left."

"Really?" Tommy turned on his stomach and carefully reached for the camera. Then he lay very still. "Okay, Tommy," Tina called. "Crawl along the

net to the ramp here. We'll help you climb back up."

But there was no answer. Tommy was still face-down in the net.

"What's the matter?" Wilson asked.

Tommy's voice shook. "Nothing's the matter," he said. "I'm fine—at least I was fine till I looked down."

"So don't look down," Annie urged. "Just look forward and start inching towards us."

But Tommy stayed where he was, his face was very pale. "I'm afraid to move," he said.

Wilson sighed. "We'll have to go down and get him."

"How are we going to do that, man?" Pablo asked.

Wilson leaned over the edge of the ramp to check the netting. "I think we can make a human chain. You stay up here," he told Pablo. "You're the biggest. You can help pull us up."

Tina peered over at the long drop below the net. She wasn't happy about Wilson's idea.

"We have no choice," Annie said.

Pablo helped Annie over the side. Then came Tina. Wilson went last.

Tina climbed down past Annie. She held onto the net and onto her friend's legs.

Wilson went down the farthest. Holding onto the net with one hand, he could just reach Tommy with the other. "Hey, man," he said, "what are you doing with that camera?"

Tina could hear a whirring noise below her. She couldn't believe what she saw! Tommy might be scared stiff, but that didn't stop him from videotaping

his friends as they tried to save him!

Wilson stretched out his hand. Tommy kept taping till the moment their hands met. Then he hung the camera around his neck. Tommy crawled up the human chain, holding onto each of the other kids with one hand. He used his other hand to pull himself along the net. When Tommy reached Annie, Pablo leaned down and grabbed his wrists. Pablo pulled Tommy up to safety. Then he helped the other three back up.

It was almost six o'clock before all five kids were back on the ramp.

Annie, Pablo, Wilson and Tina confronted Tommy. They all talked at once.

"Are you crazy, man?"

"What were you doing?"

"You could have been hurt, maybe worse!"

"Yeah, and what about us?"

"Now we don't have time to shoot anything else!" Annie added. "Tommy, how could you—"

"Don't sweat it," Tommy said, tapping the camera. "I had the camera on when I began to fall. And I got a thrilling rescue on tape. With footage like that, we're sure to win." He looked unmoved. The others angrily turned away.

"Let's at least get back to the station,"

Annie huffed. They headed for the car.

Pablo's car was parked at the ferry landing nearby. The five piled in. They reached the offices of WQSN just at the deadline. Annie wrote down the places they'd been as Tommy handed over the tape.

Mr. Hanley was not happy as he looked over the list. "There are only five places here," he said.

"But there are three dynamite scenes," Tommy said. "I taped the crypt of St. John's Church and the lost subway station. And my shots at the Harborside Bridge can count as two places. I reached the top of the tower, or near it. And then there's underneath the bridge, the safety net that I, um, fell into."

Mr. Hanley stared at him. "You fell off the bridge?"

"I even filmed my own rescue!" Tommy said proudly.

The newsman tapped his fingers on the tape box. "I'll be very interested in this," he said.

"See?" Tommy said on the way home. "Mr. Hanley is going to love our tape!"

Annie shook her head. "He didn't sound too happy."

"Well, I think he did," Tommy replied. "Besides, he's only one of the judges."

The Video Quest winners would be announced the next Saturday. Tina spent a long week waiting.

Finally, Saturday came. At the end of the evening news, Mr. Hanley sat with a pile of tapes on his desk.

"We learned a lot from our first video contest," the newsman said from the TV screen. "We need stronger safety rules, for one thing. It seems some teams thought this was a 'most dangerous video' contest."

The screen showed a whirling, out-of-focus scene that quickly went black. "Thomas Colon turned in this tape of his fall from the Harborside Bridge," said Mr. Hanley. "We're only glad the rest of his team was able to save him."

A new picture came on. It was a blurry view of the human chain that had rescued Tommy. Tina's little sister Abbie stared at the TV screen. "Tina," she said, pointing. "You're on TV!"

Another scene appeared. Wilson Chu was laughing as he seemed to tie a flag to the top of Webster Tower. "Mr. Colon

could learn a lot from his teammate
Tina Rowan," Mr. Hanley's voice said.
"He could learn safety—and how to
handle a video camera."

The news report finished. But the
night was just beginning for Tina. Her
phone started ringing off the hook.

By Monday the excitement was over,
and so was spring vacation. Tina and

Annie walked to school together.

"Well, we didn't win any prizes," Annie sighed. "But at least we were on TV after all."

Tina laughed. "I'll bet Tommy will be selling his autograph as a TV star."

But Tommy was oddly quiet when they saw him at lunch. "My dad wasn't so happy when he saw those pieces of

our videotape. I should say, my pieces of our tape." He sighed. "Looks like I'm grounded for a couple of months."

"Too bad," Wilson said.

Tommy looked down. "It's all my own fault. Plus Dad is stuck with trying to sell a nice video camera that's not new anymore."

"Bummer," Annie said.

"But there is a bright side," Tommy told them. "The camera is going at a cheap price. Dad has me working at the store to keep me out of trouble. Between working and being grounded, I don't have time to spend any money. Maybe I could save up to buy the camera."

"Great," said Tina, feeling a bit jealous.

"Maybe I'll even go into business, taping school events. You know, safe things, like talent shows or dances or graduations," Tommy said. He smiled at Tina. "That is, if you could teach me how to use the thing. We could be partners: fifty-fifty."

Wilson, Annie, and Pablo laughed.

Tina found herself smiling. "It's a deal . . . as long as we get to keep our feet on the ground!"